Mia, Mackey and the
Outside Cats

A True Story

For Ally

Best wishes

Will Medcalf

NOVEMBER 2014

By the Same Author

MIA AND THE WOODSHED CATS

For Readers Aged 9+

ANNE DROYD AND CENTURY LODGE

ANNE DROYD AND THE HOUSE OF SHADOWS

ANNE DROYD AND THE GHOSTS OF WINTER HILL

For Young Adults

THE BLUEPRINT

Mia, Mackey and the Outside Cats

A True Story

By Will Hadcroft

Illustrated by Owen Claxton

FABULOUS BOOKS

www.fbs-publishing.co.uk

First Published in the UK October 2014 by FBS Publishing Ltd.
22 Dereham Road, Thetford,
Norfolk. IP25 6ER

ISBN: **978-0-9560537-5-6**

Text Copyright © Will Hadcroft 2014
Illustration Copyright © Owen Claxton 2014
The right of William Hadcroft and Owen Claxton to be identified as the author
and illustrator of this work has been asserted by them in accordance with the
Copyright, Designs and Patents Act 1988.

Cover Design and Illustrations by Owen Claxton
Text Edited by Alasdair McKenzie
Typesetting by John Ainsworth

Paper stock used is natural, recyclable and made from wood grown in sustainable
forests. The manufacturing processes conform to environmental regulations.

*For Carol
with love*

Above:
Mia and Mackey watch as Tabby Girl
and Socks appear at the back door.

CONTENTS

Chapter One

Kittens Old and New

 Ma and Pa Croft discovered a wild cat when it kept visiting their old farm cottage one summer. It was living in the stone shed next door that the local farmer used for storing wood.

Ma called the cat Mia because it sounded like Meow.

In time, they saw that Mia had had three kittens, whose faces would appear at the woodshed window. Two, a boy and a girl, were tabby cats, their coats being a mixture of black and a dirty brown. Ma called the boy Tigger and the girl Tabby Girl.

The third one was the odd one out, because it didn't have the black and gold colouring of a tabby – no, this one was black and white with green eyes. Her gangly legs were completely black while her feet were white, as though she was wearing white socks. And so, Ma named her Socks.

Ma and Pa and their grown-up son Paul would feed Mia and the woodshed cats every day.

On one terrible occasion, Tabby Girl was hit by a car. Her tail was badly damaged, and the vet had to cut it off.

When caring for all the cats became too much for Ma and Pa, Paul took Tigger to the safari park where he worked so Tigger could live there and catch mice in their barn.

Then Mia decided she would rather live in Ma and Pa's house, because she knew something they didn't – she was going to have more babies.

And so it was on September 26 that Mia gave birth to four tiny, tiny kittens.

'Oh, look, Pa!' Ma said, bending down to examine the little black creatures snuggling up to Mia's tummy. 'They are the same size as my thumb.'

Pa smiled as one of them squeaked. 'Their eyes are shut tight,' he said.

Each morning, Ma and Pa would look in on Mia and her kittens in the basket at the top of the stairs to make sure they were all right.

Then Ma would scrape out a can of meat onto a plate for Mia's first litter, Tabby Girl and Socks, who came to the kitchen back door as soon as they knew people were about.

They gratefully lapped up the food, but were timid of entering the house. Perhaps they hadn't forgotten the time Paul caught them and took them to the vets to have operations so they wouldn't have babies. And, of course, Tabby Girl had to have her damaged tail removed. So, it was little wonder she was cautious.

The four tiny blobs that were the new kittens were fed by sucking on their mother's teats and getting milk from them. It would be months before they could eat meat.

Once, Ma Croft caught Mia picking up one of her kittens with her mouth. Although her teeth were sharp, she was gentle. She ran down the stairs with her baby in her mouth and made for the back door. Ma guessed she was trying to get her new babies to the woodshed, where the others had been born.

Ma ran up the stairs to meet her. 'No, no, darling,' she said. 'Don't take them outside.'

Mia turned around and went back upstairs to her basket and carefully lowered her kitten inside.

This happened two or three times, but each time, Ma stopped her. It was safer for the new kittens to grow up in the cottage.

As the kittens got bigger, the colouring on their coats became more obvious. They were all tabbies, some lighter than others, but each with the same pattern.

After a while, the basket at the top of the stairs was too small to fit Mia and her four babies inside it. On his day off from work, Paul brought into the cottage the cage that had been used to trap Tabby Girl and Socks to take them to the vets.

Now the cage was going to be the new home of the four kittens. Ma put towels and blankets in it, and the top was kept open so Mia could jump in and take care of them.

At night-time, a blanket was thrown over the cage so the kittens could settle and sleep.

One morning, Ma got a fork, a can of cat food and a can opener, and opened the back door to go out to feed Socks and Tabby Girl. Eager to eat her breakfast, Socks pushed herself through the gap as soon as there was enough room.

Tabby Girl, who was always nervous, stayed behind her in the yard.

'Hello, Socksey' Ma said. 'Have you come for your breakfast?'

Socks rubbed herself up against Ma's leg and purred with delight. That was a good sign, Ma thought, as it meant that Socks was getting used to being around her.

But, once Mia realised Socks and Tabby Girl were at the door, down the stairs she came. She stood behind Ma, hissing and spitting at Socks.

'Mia!' Ma called. 'Don't be horrid! Socks isn't going to get your babies. She's just here for her food.'

Ma quickly slipped through the door and shut it behind her. She knelt down on the cold floor, and emptied the tin of cat food onto the plate. As soon as she was clear, Socks and Tabby Girl rushed to it and gobbled up their breakfast.

After some weeks, Paul moved the cage carrying the new kittens into the living room so they could be where the people were.

Squeaking as loudly as they could, each of them scrambled up the bars of the cage, hoping to get out.

They would get so far and then lose their grip and fall back onto the blanket. This made everybody laugh.

One night, Ma and Pa were watching a film on television and the coal fire was blazing away in its hearth. It was a lovely, cosy evening. But they couldn't hear the television because of all the squeaking and the rattling of metal.

Pa looked at the cage. 'I think they want to come out,' he said.

'Do you think it is safe for them?'

'If we shut the middle door and make sure Mia can see them, they will be all right.'

Ma called upstairs to Paul, who was playing a computer game in his bedroom. 'We're going to let the kittens out!' she said.

Paul very rarely left his computer game for anything, but when he knew the kittens were coming out, he came downstairs to watch them.

Pa opened the lid and lowered his arm. One of the kittens grabbed hold of it with its little paws.

'Ee, ee, ee,' the kitten said.

Pa slowly lifted it; careful to make sure it didn't lose its grip and fall, and then placed it on the carpet.

Slightly stunned, the kitten looked around the room, as if it couldn't quite believe it was out and free.

Paul lifted out one of the others, and Ma took a third. Finally, Pa reached in again and cupped his hand beneath the tummy of the remaining one and gently brought it out.

Pa opened the lid and lowered his arm. One of the kittens grabbed hold of it with its little paws.

Once all four kittens were on the carpet, they began running about. Mia watched over them from her bed by the fireplace, and Ma made sure the kittens didn't go near the fire itself.

Paul never went back to finish his computer game, and Pa gave up watching his film.

Mia and her four kittens were much more entertaining!

Chapter Two

Names for the Babies

 Pa stopped the car and got out. He took the two heavy bags of shopping from the boot while Ma unlocked the front door of the cottage.

As soon as the inner door was opened and the couple stepped into the living room, Mia jumped from the settee to greet them.

Ma bent down and patted her. 'Hello, Mia.'

Mia stayed for a second, purring, before striding off, her nose in the air. She only liked a little contact with human beings because, deep down, she was still wild and feral.

Pa staggered in with the bags. 'Once we've put the shopping away,' he told Mia, 'I'll get you your surprise. We've bought you a proper bed. It's black and gold, like you, and it's in the boot of the car. You can keep it in here.'

There was a lot of rattling and squeaking coming from something near their feet.

It was the cage. Ma threw back the blanket to reveal four cute kittens – two light in shade, two dark, but all tabbies, climbing the bars of their prison.

'Hello, babies!' Ma called.

'Look at them!' Pa said. 'They are trying to get out!'

'We'll let them out once we've put the shopping away.'

Ma brewed a pot of tea and put everything away. Once she had her slippers on and was sitting on her favourite chair, Pa opened the cage and reached in.

At once, one of the lighter coloured kittens clung onto his arm, happy to be lifted out and gently placed on the floor.

When he lowered his arm inside a second time, all three remaining kittens clambered to get on. He lifted his arm, and the three of them went up in one go – and once they were out, they were all over the place.

Mia was sitting in her bed, watching her children playing. All four of them climbed up onto the basket that contained firewood. One of them crawled over the wood, while the other three swung on the handle.

A dark one pawed one of its siblings, and it toppled to the floor. But no sooner had it had landed than it was back up!

After a few minutes, two of the kittens found their way to the back of the television. Pa looked over the top of it to make sure they weren't getting tangled up in the wires.

Ma got up to go into the kitchen to make a pot of tea. As soon as she opened the door, three of the four kittens had run onto the hard tiled floor.

Ma poured piping hot water from the kettle into the teapot. She went to the fridge and brought out a bottle of milk. As she took two cups from the cupboard, she felt sharp pinpricks in her legs.

'Ow!' Ma winced. The pinpricks were moving up to her knees now. 'Ow! Ow! Ow!'

Still arranging her cups and making them ready, she looked down at the little creature clinging to her upper leg. It hung on for dear life and looked up into her face.

'Ee, ee, ee, ee, ee, ee, ee, ee!' it said.

Ma started laughing. 'What are you doing there?' she said. 'You daft thing!'

The kitten held onto her the whole time that she brewed the pot of tea. She poured two cups and dropped a little milk into both of them. She tiptoed across the kitchen to the fridge to put the milk away, careful not to tread on the other kittens that were running about and climbing up everything they could.

Eventually, Ma carefully plucked the kitten from her trousers and placed it back on the floor. She took Pa his tea.

'We could do with some names,' Pa said, 'so we don't get them mixed up.'

Ma sat in her chair. She watched Mia, who was now cleaning herself with her tongue, the way cats do.

A light grey kitten ran into the living room, followed by a darker one, and the other light one. The fourth one was charging at them from the back.

Pa laughed. 'They're chasing one another!'

The kittens ran round and round the room, round the back of the settee, then round the back of the television, and onto the wood basket again, where they swung on the handle.

'I can't tell which ones are boys and which ones are girls,' Ma said,' so it's hard to come up with names.' She studied them closely. 'I think that lighter one is a boy, so I'll call him Timmy. That was the one that climbed up my leg. The smaller light one is a girl, I think. I'll call her Scarlet. The darker one is a girl, so I'll call her Eva.'

'What about the darkest one?' Pa asked.

'I think that's a boy.'

They swung on the handle of the wood basket.

'I can't think of a proper name yet,' Ma said, 'so for now I'll just call him Blackie, because he's almost completely black.'

'You might find that he will get a bit lighter in colour when he's grown bigger,' Pa advised.

'Yes,' Ma said. 'We'll give him a proper name then.'

When dinner time came, Timmy, Scarlet, Eva and Blackie pushed themselves into Mia's bed and up to the teats on her tummy. Mia purred as they drank the special milk made by her teats. The kittens were too small to eat meat and cat food for grown-up cats.

'I think I will feed the outside cats while this lot are busy!' Ma said.

She went back to the kitchen and opened a can of food. As she got to the back door with the open can in one hand and the bowl and fork in the other, she could hear Socks and Tabby Girl meowing outside. They were waiting for her!

Ma opened the door and rushed through it before either cat could get inside. She couldn't risk them seeing Mia's new babies. She thought they might get jealous and attack them.

Socks wove herself around Ma's legs as she walked to the middle of the yard. Socks pressed herself against her and purred, happy to be fed.

Tabby Girl was standing a short distance away, nervous of human contact. Perhaps she hadn't got over all the awful things that had happened to her.

When Ma went back inside the house, Pa pointed at Mia's bed. Two of the little kittens had fallen asleep by their mother's tummy, full up with her milk.

Eva had crawled across to the rug and had fallen asleep on that. And Blackie had climbed up onto the settee and was curled up fast asleep on there.

'I think it's time to put them back in their cage,' Ma said.

Smiling, Pa got up from his armchair and carefully lifted Timmy and Scarlet from their mother's bed and gently lowered them into the cage.

With a tender grip, Ma lifted Eva from the rug and then Blackie from the settee and placed them in the cage.

Quietly, so as not to wake them, Ma slowly lowered the lid of the cage and clicked it shut. She rolled the blanket across the top so it would be nice and dark for them.

'Night, night, babies,' Ma said.

Chapter Three

Five Become Two

Paul had read on the Internet that the best time to give away kittens is 12 to 13 weeks after their birth, when they have started eating proper cat food and are ready for their injections. If they kept them any longer than that, the kittens would fret and worry too much about living in a new home.

And so Ma and Pa started thinking about whom they might give the four kittens to.

The trouble was, they had grown to love the kittens very much and didn't really want to give them away. But at the same time, they knew that once the kittens had grown to full size, they wouldn't be able to afford the food needed to care for seven cats.

Timmy, Eva, Scarlet and Blackie had grown so big now that they could be let out of their cage and left to play. Ma and Pa would watch television while the kittens chased one another in and out of the kitchen and even up and down the stairs!

Barrum, barrum, barrum! – they would go, up the stairs.

Barrum, barrum, barrum! – they would go, across the landing.

Barrum, barrum, barrum! – they would go, down the stairs.

Sometimes they would climb up onto the kitchen table or onto the worktops. Blackie liked to sit on the window sill and watch Pa do the washing up. He would scramble up the deckchair perched like a ladder between the washing machine and the sink and try to catch the bubbles with his paw.

'I thought cats were supposed to be frightened of water!' Pa would call to Ma, and then laugh.

Blackie liked to sit on the window sill
and watch Pa do the washing up.

One afternoon, Ma's friend Barbara came round to see which kitten she would like. She thought Timmy was really a girl and so she chose him. When she got him home, she changed his name to a girl's name. But after taking him to the vets, she found out he was really a boy. She didn't want to call him Timmy, though, so she changed his name to Blue.

After he had left Ma and Pa's house, Mia was very upset. She walked around all the rooms looking for him. Then she went on the living room window sill to see if she might find him outside

She jumped off the window sill and sat at Ma's feet. 'Meowww!' she said.

Ma patted her head. 'I know,' she said. 'But he couldn't stay here forever. He has gone to a good home.'

Ma's niece Lilyann said she would love to take care of Eva. And so, one Saturday afternoon, Ma and Pa put Eva on a blanket in a carrier cage. Pa got in the driver's seat of their car, and Ma rested Eva's cage on her knee.

Eva was scared. As the car drove down the road, Eva kept standing up and sitting down. She did this because she was frightened by the engine noise and the movement of the car. She didn't understand what was happening.

She meowed and meowed all the way there.

'Shhh,' Ma said. 'It's all right. We are taking you to live at Lilyann's.'

Then there was an awful smell inside the car. Pa pulled his face. 'Pooh!' he said. 'I think someone has just done something in their cage!'

'Awww,' Ma said. 'It's because she's scared.'

When they got to Lilyann's and opened the cage, Eva ran straight out of it. She was confused because she wasn't back at Ma and Pa's house. She was in a room she didn't know.

Lilyann clasped her hands together. 'Oh, she's so sweet. I love her already.'

When Ma and Pa got back home with their empty cage, Mia was upset. She paced about the house wondering where Eva had gone.

'Eva is fine,' Ma told her. 'Lilyann will look after her.'

A few days later, Pa told Ma, 'There is a man I know called Adam. His girlfriend is interested in having Scarlet.'

'And I know a young woman called Katie who is interested in having Blackie,' Ma said.

On a day that they arranged, Ma and Pa put Scarlet into the carrier cage and drove to Adam's. She cried all the way there, like Eva before her.

When they arrived, Adam made Ma and Pa a cup of tea, while his girlfriend Melissa picked up Scarlet in her hands.

'Oh!' she said. 'I can't believe how tiny she is!'

'She was even tinier than that a few weeks ago,' Pa said.

Ma and Pa drove back home, and Mia was upset again. There was only Blackie left now. It seemed strange, not having all the kittens running about. They had to get used to the house being quiet.

Some days later, Ma came home with some news. 'The girl I told you about – Katie – well, her mum says she can't afford to look after a kitten, so she can't have Blackie.'

Pa looked down at Blackie, who was climbing on the wood basket. Then he watched Mia sitting on the armchair. She was watching her baby boy climbing and having fun.

'I don't think I can stand taking him away from Mia,' Pa said. 'And I've got so used to having more than one cat in the house.'

'I feel the same,' Ma said. 'So are we keeping Blackie, then?'

'I think we should.'

Feeling very happy, Ma called upstairs to Paul. 'We've made a decision. We're keeping Blackie!'

'That's great,' Paul said.

Now that they knew Blackie was staying, they had to take Mia to the vets for the operation that would stop her having more babies. Otherwise they would end up going through it all again.

Mia handled the trip in the car better than her kittens had because she was older. The vet gave her an injection to make her fall asleep so she wouldn't feel the operation.

When Ma and Pa went back to pick her up, she was very dopey. There was a big patch of fur that had been shaved off her tummy, and on her bare skin, a line of stitches where the operation had been done.

Unlike Tabby Girl and Socks, Mia did not have one of her ears clipped to warn members of staff at the vets that she was wild. Mia had lived with Ma and Pa in their house for so long that she had become completely tame.

Once Mia was home and settled, Ma and Pa took Blackie to the vets. He had to have an injection that would stop him catching diseases from the field and animals outside the house and getting ill.

Blackie hated travelling in the car. He paced about in his carrier. He stood up and sat down, and turned around. He didn't like the noise of the engine or the movement. Like his sisters before him, he meowed all the way there.

The vet, a lady with a Scottish accent, picked him up and put him on her table.

'Oh,' she said, 'you're a bonny wee kitten, aren't you?'

Blackie walked about on her table. He sniffed her white coat and he sniffed her computer.

The vet got the injection ready. 'Let's get this over with,' she said. She pinched the scruff of Blackie's neck and stuck the needle in. With her thumb, she pressed the plunger, and the drugs that would fight off diseases went down the needle and into Blackie's body.

He didn't cry or wince, which surprised Ma and Pa.

The vet took out the needle and stroked Blackie's head.

'Now then,' she said to Ma and Pa. 'What can I tell you? He's very healthy. Judging by the colour of his fur coat, he is a mackerel tabby. And we recommend that he has his special operation to stop him chasing girl cats very soon – because if you don't, when he starts going outside, he could be gone for days and maybe get lost or have an accident on the road.'

'Okay,' Ma said, thinking about what happened when Tabby Girl got run over. 'We'll bring him back in a couple of weeks for the operation.'

When they got home, Ma told Paul, 'Blackie is what they call a mackerel tabby, because his colour is like that of a mackerel fish.'

'We can't keep calling him Blackie now we are keeping him,' Pa said. 'He needs a proper name.'

'You're right,' Ma said.

'So what are you going to call him, then?'

Ma folded her arms. 'Why don't you think of a name this time?'

'Me?'

'Yes, you think of a name for him.'

Pa stroked his chin the way he always did when he was thinking. 'Hmm,' he said. 'Let's see. Well, what do we know about him? He's a mackerel tabby, the vet said. So, we could call him Mack – short for Mackerel – or Mackey.'

'Mackey! Oh yes, I like that,' Ma said.

Pa smiled. He knelt down and tickled the kitten's chin. The little cat purred with delight.

'From now on, Blackie,' Pa told him, 'your name is Mackey.'

Chapter Four

The Things Mackey Loved

 'There we go,' Ma said. She placed a grey cat bed next to Mia's golden one by the basket of firewood in the living room. 'You now have a bed each.'

Mia was stalking about the house. She could not find Mackey anywhere.

Where was he?

Was he behind the settee? Mia looked behind the settee. He wasn't there.

Was he on the kitchen table? She jumped up onto

the table. He wasn't there.

Mia ran upstairs and peered round the door of Paul's bedroom. Was Mackey in there?

She jumped on his bed, and then crawled underneath it. He wasn't there.

Then Mia walked into the bathroom. The panel on the side of the bath was dislodged. She pulled at the corner with her teeth and the panel rattled open. Her eyes adjusted to the darkness as she crept underneath the bath.

Mackey was not there.

Finally, Mia went into Ma and Pa's bedroom. Ma was sitting on the edge of the bed, peering into a mirror on the dressing table and marking her eyelids with eyeliner.

'Hello, Mia,' Ma said.

Mia looked underneath Ma's bed. Mackey wasn't there.

There were a number of bags and cases stacked against a wardrobe. They could be used as steps, the way Mackey climbed up the deckchair that rested against the sink units to watch Pa do the washing up.

Mia leapt up onto the first bag, and from there onto the suitcase. But, as she turned to jump behind the wardrobe, Mackey shot out from the other side and ran under the bed.

With lightning speed, Mia darted after him, under the bed and out the other side, down the stairs, and into the living room. The sound of their feet on the stairs went –

Barrum, barrum, barrum, barrum!

Ma chuckled to herself, delighted by the game of hide-and-seek.

Downstairs, Pa was filling the kitchen sink with

water. He squirted washing up liquid into the rushing water to create bubbly foam.

Pa began lowering bowls, plates and a milk pan into the water, all from breakfast time.

At the sound of rushing water, Mackey's ears pricked up. Excited, he ran from the living room and straight to the deckchair propped between the washing machine and the sink unit. He scrambled up the deckchair as though it was a ladder and stepped across to the window sill.

Pa turned off the water. Taking a cloth, he washed the first plate, wiping egg stains into the soapy suds. As the water splashed, Mackey pawed the bubbles.

Pa laughed. 'What are you doing? You daft thing!' he said.

Once Pa had finished washing up and had emptied the sink, Mackey ran back upstairs.

His feet went – barrum, barrum, barrum, barrum! – on the stairs.

He went into the bathroom. His eyes were dazzled at the brand new toilet roll Ma had put in the holder. He stood up on his hind legs and grabbed the roll with his front paws. Once steady, he sank his teeth into the tissue paper and ripped it apart. Shreds of tissue floated to the floor.

Bored with the toilet roll, he went to the side panel on the bath and pulled it open. He squeezed through the narrow gap and into the darkness inside. He loved it.

After a few minutes, Mia came up looking for him. This time, she found him straight away.

He pushed himself out from under the bath and ran back downstairs, with Mia in hot pursuit –

Barrum, barrum, barrum, barrum!

*He stood up on his hind legs and grabbed
the roll with his front paws.*

In the afternoon, Ma and Pa were visited by their friend, Gerry. He took off his shoes and sat in the armchair next to Pa.

Ma was sitting on the settee, and Mia, now tired by all the running around, curled up in her bed and went to sleep.

Mackey, while sleepy, lay on his tummy and watched Gerry's toes wiggling about in his socks. He was fascinated by them.

'So, how have you been keeping?' Gerry asked, his toes twitching and wiggling.

'We're fine,' Ma said. 'We were overrun with kittens a while back, but we've given three of them away. Now we've just got Mackey and Mia.'

'Oh, I like their names,' Gerry said with a smile.

'Mia comes from "meow",' Pa explained, 'and Mackey is short for mackerel tabby, his breed.'

'Ha-ha! I like it!' Gerry said. He scrunched his toes up and tapped the carpet with the tips of his big ones and then relaxed them.

Ma said, 'It took Mia a while to get over the others going. It was awful watching her pacing about.'

'Aw,' Gerry said. 'Did she pine for them?'

'Yes. So we were glad when the girl who was going to take Mackey changed her mind.'

'Ah, yes. I suppose it's good for one of them to stay – to keep Mia company, if nothing else.'

Pa leaned across the arm of his chair. 'We will be going on holiday soon,' he said. 'I wonder how they will cope with that.'

'Paul will still be here,' Ma said quickly, 'so they won't be on their own.'

Gerry smiled at Mackey, who was staring at Gerry's twitching feet.

Gerry laughed. 'He's a character, isn't he?'

'You can say that again!' Pa said. 'He rips up toilet rolls and leaves the paper in shreds all over the bathroom floor, and pulls open the side of the bath and goes inside.'

Gerry chuckled. 'What for?'

'We're not sure. But he loves it.'

Highly amused, Gerry let out a loud laugh, his toes wiggling away.

Well, Mackey could no longer resist them. He launched forward and grabbed one of Gerry's big toes in his paws and began biting it.

Gerry jumped and the kitten's claws gripped his toe. The little teeth nibbled on his sock. It hurt and tickled at the same time.

'Ow!' Gerry exclaimed, and then laughed all the more.

Ma sprung from the settee and took the cat in her hands. 'Mackey! Leave Gerry's toe alone!'

But Gerry wasn't bothered at all. He thought it was hilarious.

Once Gerry had gone home, Mackey settled down in his bed next to his mum's. Worn out by all the excitement, he curled up. Shielding his eyes from the sunlight with his paws, it wasn't long before he was sound asleep.

Chapter Five

The Cat Flap

Ma went into the kitchen to make a cup of tea. She filled the kettle with water, and then stopped. She could hear something.

'Ee, ee, ee, ee.'

It was coming from the back door.

Ma turned the kettle on and stood by the back door.

'Ee, ee, ee, ee.'

Ma smiled and said, 'Hello babies.'

The squeaking got louder.

'Ee, ee, ee, ee!'

Ma looked over her shoulder to the open inner door leading to the living room. She knew she would have to close it if she was going to let the outside cats in.

After shutting the inner door, she opened the back door, and immediately the cats were running in and out the cottage in a frenzy – in and out, in and out – excited to be fed and frightened of being caught, all at once.

Ma opened a tin of food and gave it to them. She then poured out a plate of milk. Socks and Tabby Girl lapped it up.

There was a bumping and scuffing on the glass of the inner door. It was Mia. She was scratching the glass with her claws and meowing. Ma ignored her, allowing the cats to eat.

Mia scratched at the floor, trying to dig a tunnel out of the living room into the kitchen. She wanted to drive out the cats.

'Ignore her,' Ma said when she saw them looking nervously at the door. 'She's just trying to protect Mackey.'

Socks and Tabby Girl returned to their plate of food. Watching them, Ma saw that their fur had grown back around the area of their tummies where they'd had their operations a few months before. Tabby Girl's docked tail was just a stump, but healthy and covered in a black and dirty grey fur.

Ma knelt down and slowly reached out to Socks. The black and white cat instinctively stepped back.

'It's okay,' Ma said. She rubbed her forefinger and thumb together. 'Come on.'

Socks's big green eyes focused on Ma's hand. 'Meow,' she said.

Ma stretched her hand a little more, almost falling forward.

Socks stepped forward a single pace and extended her paw. She touched Ma's finger once and then shrank back.

'Aw,' Ma said. When she got to her feet, she felt dizzy, the blood gathering in her legs now rushing up to her head.

As soon as Ma moved, Socks ran for the open back door. Startled by the sudden movement, Tabby Girl scrambled even faster.

Ma went to close the back door. Tabby Girl and Socks were standing just outside it, side by side, looking up at her.

'Bye bye, Socks,' Ma said. 'Bye bye, Tabby

Girl.' She felt bad shutting the door on them, but she had no choice. She closed the door.

As soon as Ma opened the inner door, Mia charged through to the back door, hoping to chase off the intruders. She was confused when she got there. They had gone. She stared at the solid door. The sound of muffled meowing came through from the other side.

Pa, who was standing on the threshold of the living room, said, 'Doesn't she remember that they were her first kittens?'

'I think she's protecting Mackey from them,' Ma said.

'But they are her children too. Doesn't she know?'

'Maybe it's because she's made our home her home, and she doesn't want any more moving into her space.'

Pa shook his head. 'I suppose we can't understand everything about them. They are cats, not people. They have their own ways.'

After an hour or so, when Ma and Pa were watching television, Mia sat at Ma's feet, meowing. When Ma ignored her, Mia raised a paw and touched her leg.

Ma said to Pa, 'Will you let her out? I think she wants to go outside.'

Huffing because he was missing his programme, Pa got up and led Mia to the back door. 'Come on, Mia,' he said.

Pa opened the back door. Tabby Girl and Socks were nowhere to be seen. Mia sniffed the cool air as it came in through the open door.

Pa stared out into the darkness. 'Well, are you going out or not?' he asked impatiently. 'I want to get back to my programme.'

As if responding, Mia picked up a scent on the air and shot through the door.

No sooner had Mia exited than there was the sound of pattering feet on the hard kitchen floor and a blur of mackerel-coloured fur. Pa slammed the door shut before Mackey could follow his mum outside.

'Oh no you don't!' Pa said. He knew that if Mackey got outside and started exploring in the night, he might get lost, or worse, hurt.

After shutting the door, Pa said, 'I think it's time we had a cat flap put in the door, so Mia can come and go as she pleases.'

'But, Mackey would get out too,' Ma said as Pa returned to his chair.

'Not if we kept an eye on him,' Pa said. He sat down. 'Now, where are we up to?'

Ma gave a guilty smile. 'Er, the adverts have just started.'

'Brilliant,' Pa replied as the adverts played on the television. He didn't think it was brilliant that he'd missed some of his programme, of course. He was being sarcastic.

The next day, Ma decided to phone her grown-up niece Pamela to see if her son-in-law David would come with his toolbox and put a cat flap in the back door, because he'd put one in for Pamela.

Ma and Pa were thrilled when David turned up. He went to the back door, knelt down, and began measuring the shape of the hole. He drew it on with a pencil. Then he plugged in his power saw and cut the square shape out. The saw made a terrible din, and Ma had to keep the inner door closed and sit with Mia and Mackey so they wouldn't be too frightened.

Within an hour, David had finished. The back door now had a panel in it that opened both ways. Mia could go in and out as often as she pleased.

Ma paid David his wages and he left, pleased to have done his job well.

'Now then,' Pa said, opening the inner door. 'Will Mia go through it?'

Mia trotted in, curious to see what had been happening. She sniffed round the back door.

Ma got down on her haunches and pushed the flap with her finger. Cool air brushed in over her hand. 'See,' she said, looking at Mia, 'see, a flap. A little door.' She pushed it again. 'See, Mia. A little door for you.'

Mia looked at her, but didn't move.

'See,' Ma said again. She pushed the flap high up and let go to demonstrate how it swung back and forth. 'You can go outside.'

Unimpressed, Mia turned and trotted back into the living room.

Wondering what all the fuss was about, Mackey inspected the hatch, sniffing all round it. Having no idea what it was for, he too joined his mother in the living room.

'Hmm,' Pa said, stroking his chin. 'I don't think she "gets" it. I think we're going to have to pick her up and throw her through it, or something.'

Ma could hear a noise coming from outside.

'Ee, ee, ee, ee.'

She knelt down to look. Filling the square-shaped see-through plastic at the bottom of the door were two heads, one mackerel-coloured, the other black and white with green eyes.

Ma laughed. 'Hello, you two!'

She pressed her finger against the panel. The

kittens jumped back as it opened outwards. Kneeling right down, Ma put her face to the flap.

'It's a little door, see,' she said. Ma stood up, waiting for one of them to pluck up the courage to come in.

Ma laughed. 'Hello, you two!'

Nothing happened.

'I don't think they understand what it is, either!' Pa said.

Ma turned to join him in the living room, when she thought of something.

'I'd better lock it shut,' she said, 'in case Mackey figures it out in the night and goes out.' She clicked the button that locked the panel shut.

Hearing the click, two furry heads on the other side filled the clear plastic again.

Chapter Six

It's a Cat's Life

 In a spell of warm weather, Ma had been leaving the back door open during the afternoons so that Mia and Mackey could go out on the field, as they still had not grasped what the cat flap was for.

On some occasions, Tabby Girl and Socks crept in while Mia and Mackey were out, and had meat and milk!

On this day, though, it was quite cold, so Ma kept the door shut. She was sitting in the living room with Pa when she heard a click-click noise coming from the kitchen.

'What was that?' she asked.

'I'm not sure,' Pa said. He got up and went into the kitchen to look. 'I can't see anything!' he called.

Ma glanced around the room. Mia was curled up in her bed and was sleeping. But where was Mackey?

'Is Mackey in there?' she said.

'No,' came the reply. 'I can't see him.'

'Is he upstairs, then?'

'I don't think so.'

Ma smiled, getting excited. 'He must have gone through the cat flap, then!'

Pa appeared in the inner doorway. He too was excited. 'I can see him!' he blurted. 'He's out in the field!'

Ma got up to look, and there was Mackey pawing something in the middle of the field.

Probably a mole or a mouse or something, she thought.

Knowing that Mackey would likely stay on the field rather than go near the road, Ma and Pa felt secure in preparing for the visit of Pa's business partner Theresa.

Pa had written some books, and Theresa was helping him get them published. When she arrived, Pa brewed a pot of tea while Theresa chatted with Ma in the living room.

Theresa had long dark brown hair and wore a red jacket, a white blouse and a long skirt. When she sat down, she slipped off her shoes and opened one of the bags she had been carrying.

'I've brought you some different flavoured teas,' she told Ma, who inspected the bag. 'I think you will like them.'

Pa brought in a tray carrying a teapot, three cups, and a jug of milk. He placed it on the small table in the middle of the room. Pa poured tea he had already brewed into the cups and handed them out.

Once everyone was settled, Theresa opened her shoulder bag and pulled out some papers.

'Here are my plans for publishing your book,' she said.

Pa examined the plans.

A click-click noise could be heard from the kitchen.

'I think you-know-who has just come back in,' Ma said, grinning.

And sure enough, Mackey came trotting in. But there was something odd about him.

'His head is a funny colour,' Pa said. 'What is it?'

Mackey sat down near his mother, who was still

sleeping in her bed. He licked his paws and wiped his head with them.

Ma bent down and sniffed. She screwed up her face. 'Pooh!' she cried. 'He stinks!'

'What is it?'

'I think he's been pushing his face in cow muck!'

Everyone laughed at that. Mackey stopped cleaning his face and looked at them, perhaps wondering what all the laughter was about. He returned to his preening, which made everyone laugh some more.

Theresa sipped her tea and then continued showing Pa her plans for his book. As she talked, she twitched her toes. She pointed to the designs that Pa could choose from for the cover of his book. Excited by what she was telling him, she wiggled her toes even more.

'Hey, they are great!' Pa said.

Theresa smiled. 'I think we could have it published by the autumn.' She was very excited now, and her toes twitched and wiggled as she spoke.

'Ow!' Theresa shouted. She looked down at her feet.

Ma and Pa glanced down at her toes, too, and there was Mackey, his paws wrapped around Theresa's right foot and his teeth chewing on her big toe.

Ma snapped her fingers to get his attention and then tapped the floor. 'Mackey.' Tap, tap, tap. 'Mackey, come here.' In the end, she had to pull him off Theresa's foot by hand.

He wriggled himself free and jumped on the side of the chair Theresa was sitting on. His claws went into the green leather as he made his way up to the headrest, upon which was draped a cloth cover. He sat on it.

... and there was Mackey, his paws wrapped around Theresa's right foot and his teeth chewing on her big toe.

Theresa went back to her papers a third time. As she talked, her long dark hair swished about.

'Ow!' she shouted again.

Mackey was pawing her hair and getting more and more tangled up!

'My hair! My hair!' Theresa kept saying.

In the end, Ma lifted Mackey off the chair, carefully unravelled the tangle of hair from his paws and put him in the kitchen. She shut the middle door to make sure he couldn't get back in.

Mia slept through the whole thing.

After Theresa had gone, Ma and Pa went out to visit their friend Gerry. They chatted and chatted. He asked about the cats, and they brought him up to speed on all the things that had happened recently. Gerry loved hearing about them. He laughed a lot when they told him about Mackey coming in covered in cow muck.

Ma, Pa and Gerry lost track of the time as they talked and shared stories. By the time Ma and Pa got home, it was dark. Thankfully, Paul was around to keep the cats company. Mia was curled up asleep in the bed at the top of the stairs, and

Mackey was sitting on Paul's bed while Paul played a computer game.

When Ma and Pa came into the kitchen, Mackey came down the stairs, step by step, careful that his four feet didn't slip on the wood. He stopped when he was the same height as Pa, so he could look him in the face.

'Mmyeyeyeyeyeyeyeye-nyer,' Mackey said.

It sounded like Mackey was telling them off, as if he was saying, 'What time do you call this? You don't normally stay out this long. I want my dinner!'

Pa roared with laughter.

Ma took a tin of food, opened it, and scraped the contents into two bowls. She also poured out some milk. In seconds, Mackey made his way down the stairs and got stuck in. Mia trotted down after him.

'Ee, ee, ee, ee, ee, ee, ee!' came a squeak from outside.

Ma grinned. 'The outside cats.'

She opened the door, and straight away Socks and Tabby Girl were there, weaving themselves around her legs. They remained by the open door while Ma put out more food and milk.

Mia and Mackey were so busy eating their own food that they didn't bother chasing them away.

Pa stood watching, his hands on his hips. 'I don't know,' he said. 'This lot are costing us a fortune!'

Once Tabby Girl and Socks had finished eating, they walked around the kitchen, making sure they kept some distance from Mia and Mackey. Socks jumped up onto the table and then climbed into the wicker basket which Ma was now using for her washing.

'She's made herself at home!' Pa said. He smiled at the cat. 'Mackey and his brother and sisters were born in that basket, you know.'

Tabby Girl sat on the big blue cushion by the back door, ready to make a run for it if need be. She was still very nervous.

After she had finished eating, Mia became impatient, pacing about the kitchen. Tabby Girl ran into the yard straight away, and after a few minutes' resistance, Socks joined her. Ma shut the door.

Mackey trotted over to the cat flap and sat watching the cats outside. Pa bent down and pushed the pancl so it opened.

'Do you want to go out, Mackey?' Pa asked.

Mackey looked up at him. After a second, he said, 'M-neow,' then got up, and went off to the living room.

Arching his eyebrows and putting his hands on his hips, Pa said, 'I guess that means no!'

Chapter Seven

Mackey Falls and Mia Sees Red Eyes

 Paul was Ma's grown-up son. But Ma also had a grown-up daughter called Marie. Marie didn't live at Ma and Pa's house because she was married to a man named Mark.

Marie and Mark paid Ma and Pa a visit. They were excited because they had a surprise for them.

'We've booked a holiday,' Marie said, the tips of her fingers on her right hand touching those on her left, as she could barely contain her excitement. 'Me and Mark, you and Pa,' she said.

'That's fantastic!' Ma said. 'Where are we going?'

Mark raised his forefinger as though he was making a special announcement. 'To America!'

'America?'

'On a ship,' Mark said, his face beaming.

Ma was concerned that Paul wouldn't be able to go, but Paul said he didn't fancy going anyway. He would stay home and look after the cats.

Mackey loved chasing a plastic medallion on a string. Mark picked it up and trailed it across the floor. Mackey snapped down his paw, here and there, trying to catch the thread.

Ma, Pa, Mark and Marie decided to go into town and celebrate their holiday by having a meal.

While they were out, Mia curled up in her bed and went to sleep, and Mackey went upstairs to sit on Paul's bed while Paul watched television in his room.

'All right, mate?' Paul said as he saw Mackey enter the room.

Mackey jumped up onto the bed, and Paul continued with his back to him and watched television.

It was a nice sunny afternoon and Paul had opened his window a little to allow some fresh air into the room. The scents from the flowers and the smells of the farmland floated in. A cow in a distant field mooed, and a sheep bleated. Mackey's ears pricked up when he realised the window was open.

He got up, walked carefully across the uneven bedding, and got onto the window sill. He sniffed the air coming in through the open window. The smell was tempting, delicious. Mackey pushed the window with his nose.

Paul was so engrossed in his television programme he didn't hear Mackey on the window ledge. He thought he was asleep on the bed.

There was a sharp crack as something fell over, followed by a yelp. Paul glanced over his shoulder, wondering what it was. The window was wide open. He turned right round to check his bed. Mackey was no longer curled up upon it.

Paul realised what had happened and ran to the window. He stuck his head out and looked at the mackerel-coloured heap on the hard floor of the yard below. The heap moved. It was Mackey. He was slumped to one side. Pushing himself up on his front paws, he saw Paul looking out the bedroom window.

He stuck his head out and looked at the
mackerel-coloured heap on the hard
floor of the yard below.

'Mmm-nyoooooooow!' Mackey cried, and Paul understood he was in pain.

Falling out of an upstairs window was a terrible thing to happen to anybody. Mackey might have hit the pipe sticking out of the wall as he fell through the air, or he might have broken his leg or his hip when he landed on the stone floor.

Paul turned off the television, ran downstairs and yanked open the back door.

Mackey was still there, slumped to one side and pushing himself up on his front paws. He could not stand up on his back legs.

Paul knelt down and pushed his hands under Mackey's body. 'This might hurt you, mate,' he said, 'but we've got to get you to the vets.'

Paul was very worried.

By the time Ma, Pa, Mark and Marie had returned from their meal, Paul and Mackey were back from the vets.

Ma frowned as she saw the little cat limping. 'What's the matter with him? He's not walking properly.'

Paul told her what had happened and that the vet said Mackey would be all right in a few weeks. His leg was badly sprained, but the vet did not think it was broken.

Everyone was upset, but they were so glad that Mackey hadn't been killed by the fall.

Mark and Marie went home and Paul went out to work at the safari park. That night, he phoned home to make sure Mackey was okay. Ma told him he was. Paul was glad to hear it.

After the cats were fed, Pa shut the curtains in the living room. He and Ma sat down to watch a movie when Mia came in and leapt up onto the TV stand. From there she jumped onto the window sill. The curtains moved as she sat down on the other side of them.

Ma and Pa watched their movie.

The curtains moved as Mia jumped back down and ran into the kitchen. Click-click went the cat flap.

Ma and Pa watched their movie.

Minutes later, Mia came back. She jumped onto the TV stand, and from there onto the window sill. The curtains swayed a little as she sat down.

'Mmmmmm,' Mia said from behind the curtain, irritated. She jumped from the window sill, onto the TV stand, onto the floor, and ran into the kitchen. Click-click went the cat flap.

'Something's got to her,' Ma said.

Pa rose from his chair and parted the curtains with his finger. 'I wonder what it is.' He squinted at the trees and bushes across the road. It was hard to make out any detail in the dark. 'I can't see anything,' he said.

While Pa was standing, Mia rushed back in, and back onto the window sill. Her fur was ruffled. Her head twitched with agitation.

'What is it, Mia?' Pa said, following her gaze. She was focusing on something in the undergrowth across the road. It was driving her mad. And then Pa saw it himself.

There were two tiny red eyes in the shrubbery – two red eyes, watching.

'Ooh, it's weird,' Pa said. 'It's like they are looking right through me. No wonder she feels spooked.'

Ma frowned and got to her feet. 'What is it?'

Pa pointed out the two red lights in the undergrowth. 'Do you see?'

Ma shivered at the sight of them. 'Red eyes! What is it out there? A tomcat?'

There were two tiny red eyes in the shrubbery – two red eyes, watching.

'Or a fox?' Pa suggested.

Mia turned and jumped from the window sill. Whatever the creature was, it was really winding her up.

Pa closed the curtains. He and Ma returned to their film.

The following day, Ma and Pa kept an eye on Mackey. He was still very upset and shocked by what had happened to him. He slowly crawled, one step at a time, upstairs and pulled himself underneath Ma and Pa's bed. He didn't want to come out and didn't move when anyone spoke to him.

Pa got on his hands and knees and peered under the bed. 'Come on, Mackey,' he said in a soft voice. 'You can't stay under there forever.' Mackey looked at him, but didn't move.

Finally, Ma came up with a plate of food and some milk and slid them under the bed towards him.

'Mackey has been deeply affected by what happened,' she said. 'He will come out when he's ready.'

Ma and Pa went downstairs to the kitchen. They were surprised to find Socks sitting in the wicker basket on the table!

'How did she get there?' Pa asked.

'She must have come in through the cat flap.'

But she wasn't the only visitor. A mackerel-coloured cat walked nervously across the floor towards Ma. Its right ear was clipped and it had no tail.

'Hello, Tabby Girl,' Ma said. Tabby Girl brushed herself against Ma's legs. Ma bent down and stroked her.

'This is amazing!' Pa cried.

Ma fed them both. 'They're getting used to us,' she said. 'I can't believe how Tabby Girl has come on – to go from being afraid of us and running away, especially after her road accident, to coming up for a love.'

After the cats were fed, Pa closed the living room curtains, as it was getting dark, and settled down in front of the television.

Mia came into the house through the flap, ran through the kitchen, and jumped onto the living room window sill. Pa could see she was agitated again. He peered through the curtains.

The red eyes were there again!

'This is doing my head in,' Pa said. 'I'm going to go out and see what that thing is once and for all.' He put on his slippers and coat, and carefully opened the front door. He walked slowly so as not to frighten off the animal. The red eyes didn't move – they were watching him.

He felt a bit scared as he approached.

And then his fear faded away into nothing as he saw what it was. Buried deep in the shrubbery was a red Coke can. Pa looked up at the street lamp a few metres away, and then back at the can. The light was shining on the red of the can. This was what they were all seeing from the window.

Upon returning to the house, Pa stood in the living room, still wearing his slippers and coat. He held one arm behind his back. 'Well, I solved the mystery of the red eyes,' he said.

'What are they?' Ma said.

Pa brought his hand forward and held up the can.

'A Coke can?' Ma shouted. She looked at Mia. 'All that fuss for a Coke can?'

'Ee, ee,' Mia replied, and jumped from the window sill.

Ma and Pa laughed.

With the Coke can in his hand, Pa hugged his wife. They laughed again. The cats had taken over their lives.

Chapter Eight

The Invasion

Mackey's left leg was dragging slightly when he walked, but at least he was walking – and more importantly, he was out from under Ma and Pa's bed and enjoying life as he used to do.

Socks and Tabby Girl were taking their chances and sneaking into the house at different times of the day. Mia didn't like them coming in, but she would allow them to eat before she chased them off. They belonged in the woodshed, as far as she was concerned.

At the safari park, Paul looked in on Tigger. He was now as much as part of the place as the lions and tigers were.

Ma and Pa went to visit Ma's niece Lilyann. They were excited about seeing Eva after all that time. Would she even remember who they were?

When Ma and Pa arrived at Lilyann's apartment, Eva hid in the bedroom. She didn't like people she didn't know visiting. But, after a while she seemed to realise that she knew the visitors.

'She's grown so much,' Ma said.

Pa grinned. 'Well, she is Mackey's sister, born on the same day, so she will be the same size as him.'

Eva sniffed Ma's shoes.

'She will probably pick up Mackey's scent on them,' Pa said.

'Yes,' Ma agreed. 'It's like she remembers his scent more than she remembers us.'

They were pleased that Eva could barely remember them, as it meant that she wouldn't want to go back home with them. It also meant that the other kittens – Blue at Barbara's and Scarlet at Adam's – wouldn't be pining for their old lives, either.

The time came for Ma and Pa, and Mark and Marie, to go on their cruise holiday to America.

Ma began packing clothes into a suitcase in her bedroom. When Mia saw the case, she got into it and sat down.

'Do you think she realises we are going away?' Ma asked.

'Maybe,' Pa said.

'Perhaps she is trying to stop us going, or she thinks she is coming with us.'

'Could be.'

Ma knelt down and wagged a finger at Mia. 'You can't come with us, Mia, no you can't.'

'Ee, ee,' Mia said.

Ma left a list of chores for Paul to do while they were away. The main ones were to do with the cats: feed them a tin and some biscuits once in the morning and once in the afternoon. Don't forget the outside cats. Change the litter trays.

When the morning came for Ma and Pa to get their taxi to the railway station, Mia and Mackey sat in the living room and waited with them.

There was a click-click in the kitchen, followed by a second click-click. Pa went in to find Socks gobbling up some meat and Tabby Girl sitting in the wicker basket on the table.

He laughed. 'These two have definitely lost their fear. They are in and out as it pleases them, now.'

'They still see the woodshed as their home, though,' Ma said. 'We are just somewhere to visit and a place to feed.'

There was a rat-a-tat-tat on the front door as the taxi driver arrived to take them to the station. Pa slid out the handle on the big suitcase and wheeled the case to the door.

Ma picked up her bags. 'Be good, Mia and Mackey,' she said. 'We'll be back in two weeks.'

As if responding, Mia pressed herself against Ma's legs and wove herself around them.

It was going to be hard leaving Mia and Mackey behind.

Ma and Pa met Marie and Mark at the railway station. They travelled on the train down the country to Southampton and stayed there overnight in a hotel. The following day, they got on board the ship.

That evening, they sailed with hundreds of other holidaymakers from Southampton across the Atlantic Ocean towards America. It was going to take them seven days to get there.

On the third day, Pa decided to use the ship's Internet cafe to send an email to Paul at home. On the fourth day, Pa logged on to find a reply.

Paul had written that everyone was fine at home. He said that Mia and Mackey kept looking at the front door, hoping Ma and Pa were coming back. Mia sat on the window sill to look out for them.

Cats didn't understand about trips and holidays. To them, Ma and Pa had gone away and not come back. That's all they understood.

Pa got upset thinking about it. He wished there was a way he could explain it to them.

On the seventh day, the ship arrived in New York in America. Ma, Pa, Mark and Marie enjoyed walking down Seventh Avenue and Times Square. It was like walking around a movie set, with the traffic noises and the yellow taxis being just as they were in American films.

On the eighth day, they went up a huge building so they could see New York from the roof. It was amazing. They saw skyscrapers and old buildings and bridges across the river, and the Statue of Liberty in the distance. In the afternoon, they took a bike and cart ride around Central Park.

On the ninth day, they prepared to return home by aeroplane. They arrived at the airport and got the plane at 7.30 p.m. Six and a half hours later, they had landed in Manchester, England, and it was now the following morning.

Pa thought it was like travelling in time, as normally the night-time lasted much longer than six and a half hours.

After their journey on the train, Ma and Pa, and Mark and Marie, got in separate taxis.

When Ma and Pa arrived outside their cottage, and Ma paid the driver, Paul saw them through the window and came to the front door. He was very glad to see them. He was holding Mackey in his hands and stroking him.

Pa wheeled his suitcase to the door and smiled at Mackey. 'Hello, Mackey,' he said and reached out to tickle the kitten's chin.

Mackey looked at him, and then after a delay, realising who it was, started to wriggle to get free.

'I'd better put him inside the house,' Paul said.

Pa wasn't sure if Mackey was excited to see him, or if he was upset because he and his mother had been left for two weeks.

Once Ma was inside the cottage, she got on her haunches to welcome Mackey and his mother. 'Hello, my babies,' she said. But Mackey shrunk back.

Responding to the sound of human voices – voices she recognised – Mia appeared at the kitchen doorway. She stopped and looked up at Ma.

'Hello, darling,' Ma said, and reached out to stroke her.

Mia stood still and stared at her. It was as though she couldn't quite believe Ma and Pa had returned.

After an hour or so, things were more like normal. Mia and Mackey came over to be stroked.

Paul said, 'I didn't have to change the litter tray much, as they hardly used it. They spent a lot of time outside on the field.'

Pa nodded. 'They've got used to using the cat flap. That is good.'

After having a refreshing cup of tea, Ma and Pa went out in their own car to get some shopping.

'Now, we are coming back,' Ma told Mia. 'We will only be an hour.'

They had enjoyed the cruise ship and their visit to America, but they were now happy to be home. They had missed Mia, Mackey and the outside cats so much.

Returning from the shops, Ma and Pa stumbled into their cottage, their bags of shopping weighing them down.

'Hey!' Pa said, laughing. 'Will you look at this?'

Ma shut the front door and turned. 'What is it?'

They had been invaded. Mia was sitting by the hearth, watching over her little family. Mackey was in his bed by the fireplace, licking his paws and cleaning himself. Socks was lying on the rug and stretching out her long black and white legs. And Tabby Girl was curled up on the settee fast asleep.

'Charming,' Ma said.

'It looks like the outside cats have become the inside cats.'

Ma put her shopping bags on the floor. 'It does,' she said.

'You do realise that if we ever move house, this lot will have to come with us?'

'I do,' Ma said. And she wouldn't have had it any other way.

Mia was sitting by the hearth,
watching over her little family.

Next

Mia and the Farmhouse Cats

Keep up to date at *www.fbs-publishing.co.uk*

www.facebook.com/TheMiaBooks

Acknowledgments

I would like to thank the following for their support.

Jim and Marion Holden
Paul Schofield
Ruth at Vets for Pets, Astley Bridge

Special thanks to the FBS team;

For advising me on the text
Alasdair McKenzie

For creating these lovely paintings
Owen Claxton

For typesetting and graphics
John Ainsworth

For PR and bags of enthusiasm
Theresa Cutts

For her loyal support and for loving this project
my wife Carol

Mia, Mackey, Timmy, Scarlet, Eva, Tabby Girl,
Socks and Tigger really exist.
This is their real life story.

Your nearest Cats Protection centre can be found
at *www.cats.org.uk*

Also From FBS Publishing

Mia and the Woodshed Cats
By Will Hadcroft.
Illustrated by Owen Claxton

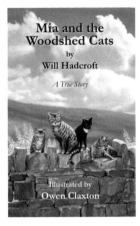 Ma and Pa Croft live with their grown up son Paul in a stone cottage in the English countryside. When a stray cat turns up,

Ma puts out some meat and milk - and then three faces appear at the woodshed window.
Kittens!

Where has the cat come from? Will Ma and Pa's landlord, the local farmer, allow the kittens to stay in the woodshed?

And what will happen to them when they've grown up?

This is the story of Mia, Tigger, Tabby Girl and Socks, and is based on real events. It's a story that will touch your heart.